To Eba

From
Mrs Palin.

Mary, Mary, Quite Contrary

Illustrations by
Henriette Willebeek Le Mair

FREDERICK WARNE

FREDERICK WARNE
Published by the Penguin Group
Penguin Books Ltd, 27 Wrights Lane, London W8 5TZ, England
Penguin Putnam Inc., 375 Hudson Street, New York, NY 10014, USA
Penguin Books Australia Ltd, Ringwood, Victoria, Australia
Penguin Books Canada Ltd, 10 Alcorn Avenue, Toronto, Ontario, Canada M4V 3B2
Penguin Books (N.Z.) Ltd, 182-190 Wairau Road, Auckland 10, New Zealand

Penguin Books Ltd, Registered Offices: Harmondsworth, Middlesex, England

Illustrations taken from *Our Old Nursery Rhymes* and *Little Songs of Long Ago*,
1911 and 1912, originally published by Augener Ltd
First published in this format 1999 by Frederick Warne

1 3 5 7 9 10 8 6 4 2

ISBN 0 7232 4553 3

Printed and bound in Singapore by Tien Wah Press (Pte) Ltd
Colour reproduction by Anglia Graphics, Bedford, England

Contents

Little Jack Horner

Little Jack Horner
    Sat in a corner,
Eating his Christmas pie;
    He put in his thumb,
    And pulled out a plum,
And said 'What a good boy am I!'

Four and Twenty Tailors

Four and twenty tailors
    Went to catch a snail,
The best man among them
    Durst not touch her tail;
She put out her horns
    Like a little Kyloe cow,
Run, tailors, run,
    Or she'll kill you all e'en now.

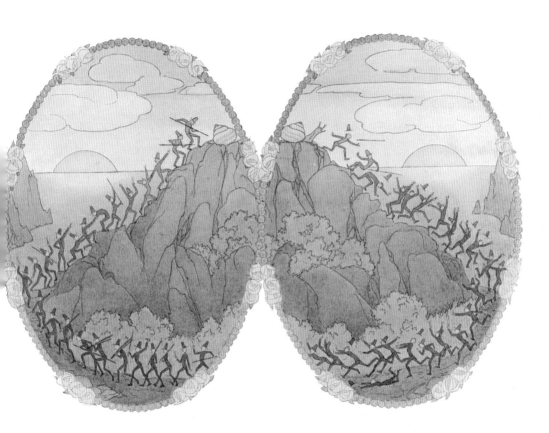

Georgie Porgie

Georgie Porgie, pudding and pie,
  Kissed the girls and made them cry;
When the boys came out to play,
  Georgie Porgie ran away.

Dance to Your Daddy

Dance to your daddy,
My little babby,
Dance to your daddy,
My little lamb!

You shall have a fishy
In a little dishy,
You shall have a fishy
When the boat comes in!

Baa, Baa, Black Sheep

Baa, baa, black sheep,
Have you any wool?
Yes, sir, yes, sir,
Three bags full;
One for the master,
One for the dame,
And one for the little boy
Who lives down the lane.

There Was a Crooked Man

There was a crooked man,
 And he walked a crooked mile,
He found a crooked sixpence
 Upon a crooked stile;
He bought a crooked cat,
 Which caught a crooked mouse,
And they all lived together
 In a little crooked house.

The Spider and the Fly

Will you walk into my parlour?
Said the spider to the fly.
    'Tis the prettiest little parlour
    That you ever did espy;
The way into my parlour
Is up a winding stair,
    And I have many pretty things
    To show you when you're there.
Oh, no, no! said the little fly,
To ask me is in vain,
    For who goes up your winding stair
    Shall ne'er come down again.

Three Little Mice Sat Down to Spin

Three little mice sat down to spin;
Pussy passed by and she peeped in.
What are you doing, my little men?
Weaving coats for Gentlemen.
Shall I come in and cut off your threads?
No, no, Mistress Pussy, you'd bite off our heads.
Oh, no, I'll not; I'll help you spin.
That may be so, but you don't come in.

Mary, Mary, Quite Contrary

Mary, Mary, quite contrary,
How does your garden grow?
With silver bells and cockle shells,
And pretty maids all in a row.

The North Wind Doth Blow

The north wind doth blow,
And we shall have snow,
And what will poor robin do then,
Poor thing?
He'll sit in a barn,
And keep himself warm,
And hide his head under his wing,
Poor thing.

Rock-a-Bye Baby

Rock-a-bye baby,
  On the tree top.
When the wind blows
  The cradle will rock;
When the bough breaks
  The cradle will fall.
Down will come baby,
  Cradle and all.